"Ahhh! What a beautiful day to be alive and well, and finished with eating _matzos_ for Passover!"

"Hey! Instead of eye of newt, how about some fat of chicken?"

"We just got a call from the _shul_ down the block. Could we find them a tenth man for a _minyan_?"

"Oh, just you wait till your patriarch gets home!"

"I love it when your eyes blaze like that; you remind me of Moses."

"Or, if you prefer, I also have lox and bagels."

"Jewish people go out for Chinese food, but do you ever see Chinese people going out for Jewish food?"

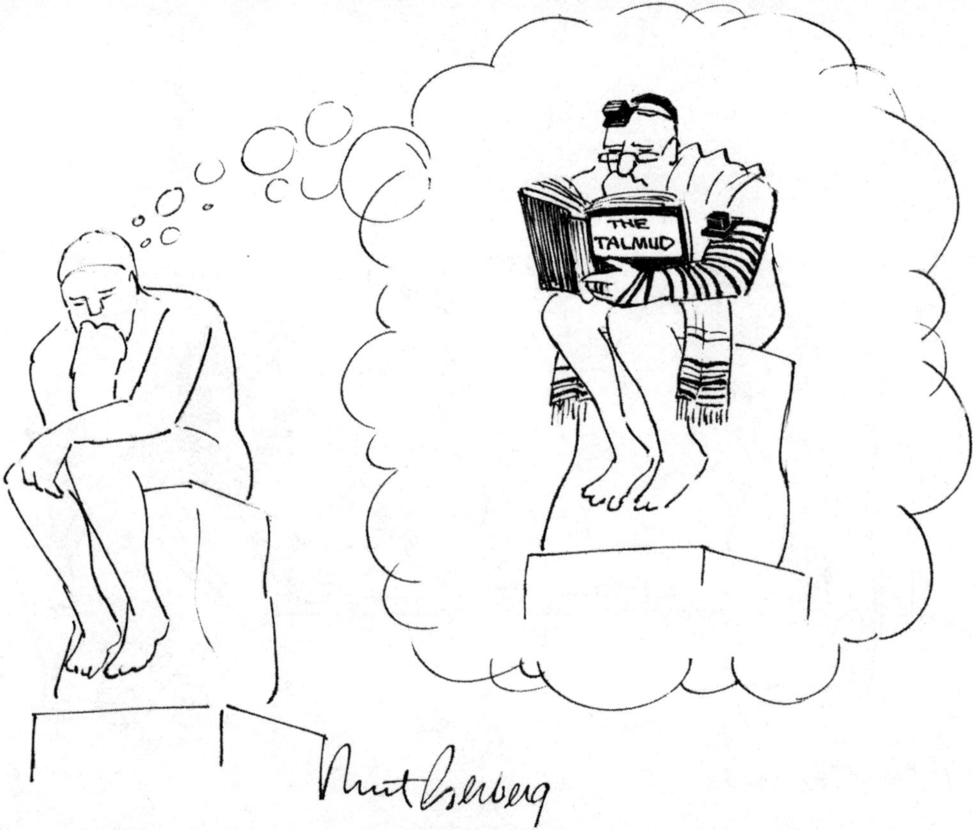
THE TALMUD

"*Great, just great!* And while you're in here, potchkeeing around with paint, Seymour Rabinowitz in the cave next door is inventing fire already!"

"What about _my_ name?"

"Height has nothing to do with it, Arnie. I just can't imagine myself with a man who doesn't know the broche for hors d'oeuvres."

AT THE AGE OF 39, SIDNEY SUSSMAN BECAME UNDENIABLY AWARE OF HIS JEWISHNESS

"I feel the need for an ethnic pick-me-up, Herb. Give me a glass of Manischewitz Concord Grape wine—straight up."

"Mr. Berkowitz, I and my Jewish career counselor, hereby wish you a <u>mazel tov</u> on your birthday."

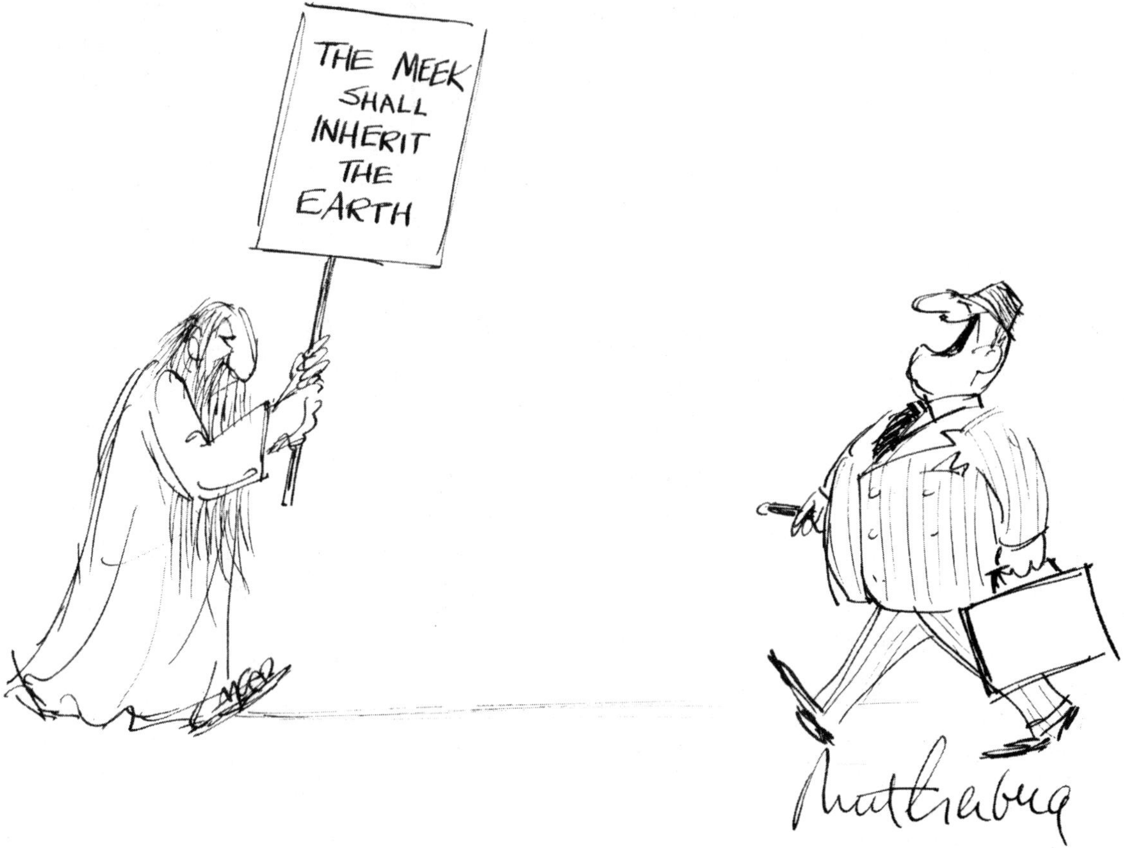
THE MEEK SHALL INHERIT THE EARTH

"It's extremely flexible. You can wear it as comfortably to Yom Kippur services as out on a date with a shiksa."

"What do you mean, 'No hot pastrami'? What kind of heaven do you call this?"

"'Seizing control'? Is that the thanks you give a parent company?!"

"It would be sweet to be your Valentine, Kevin, but the concept's too _goyish_ for me, and besides, I don't date _shaygetsers_."

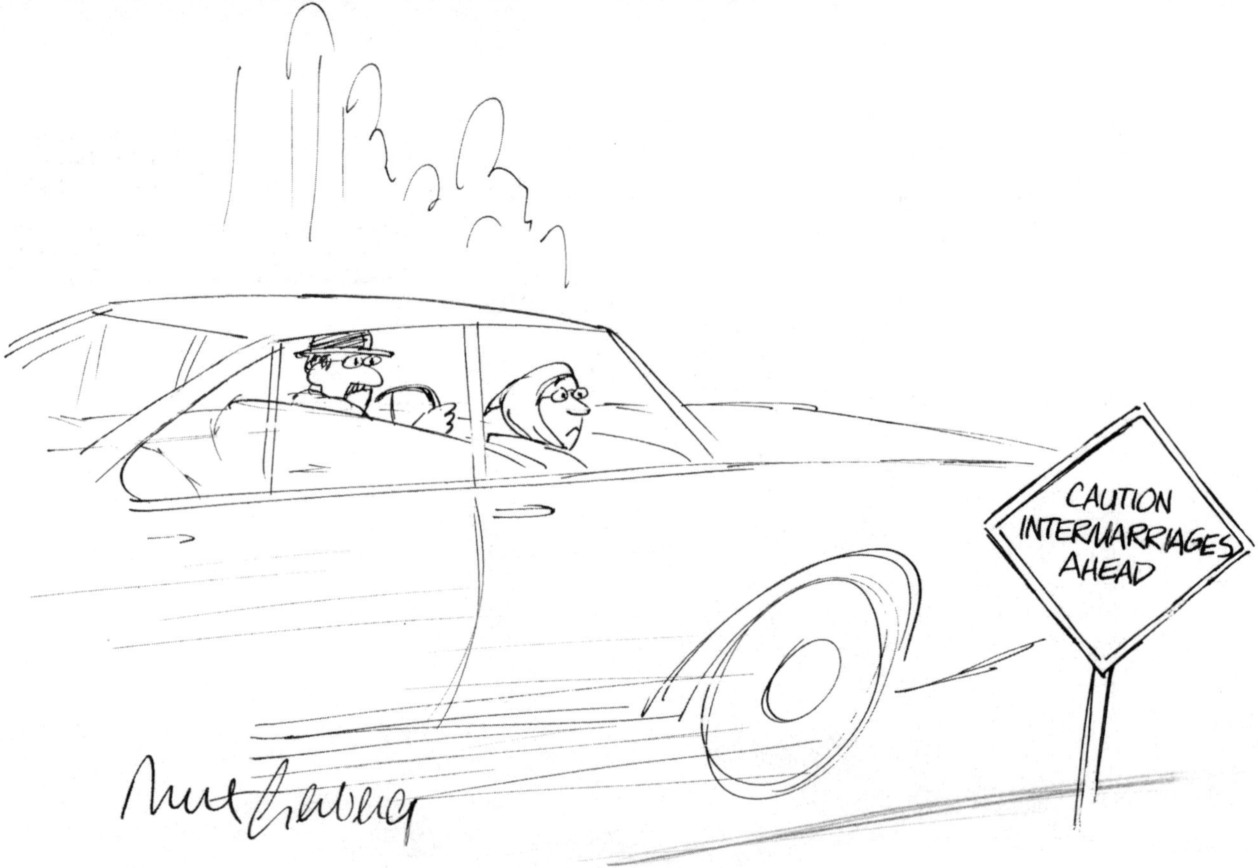
CAUTION
INTERMARRIAGES
AHEAD

ISRAEL, IRREGARDLESS

"Everybody's waiting, Miriam—hurry up and float!"

"Even when you're out on a _date_?"

BEERSHEBA
BEDOUIN
CAMEL
MARKET
PHOTOGRAPH
ON A
CAMEL
I.L. 3.00

"I don't care if this is Israel—my Grandma Flance still makes better gefilte fish!"

"I think he wants to sell us a tree to be planted in our name in Brooklyn."

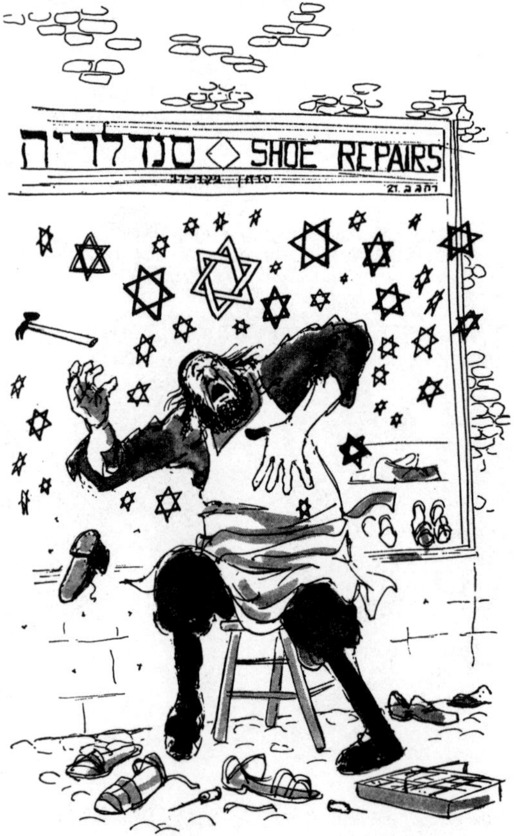
סנדלריה
SHOE REPAIRS

"... *And here you can see the plains of Judea, where David slew Goliath, a place of beauty and richness, a place of marvels and history, and a wonderful place for some businessman's branch office ...*"

"'Speeding'? This you call speeding? Listen, our Milky Way Galaxy—rushing through the universe at 600 miles a second—that's speeding!"

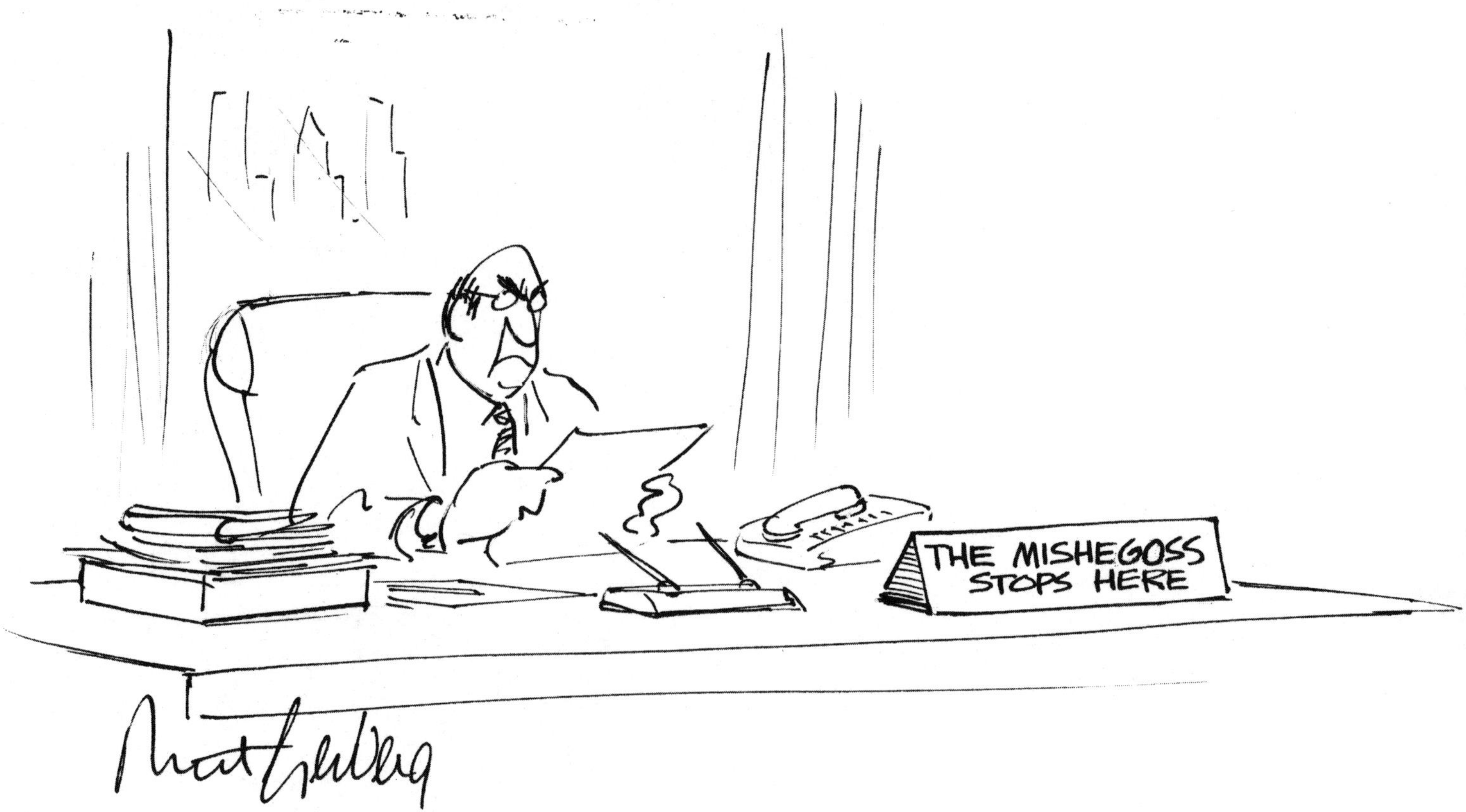
THE MISHEGOSS
STOPS HERE

"Well, Jacob, maybe if you really _tried_ to pretend I was Cybill Shepherd you _could_ pretend I was Cybill Shepherd."

"I've told you a thousand times, Rose; during Christmas, don't get into religious arguments with the goyim!"

JEWISH TIME CHECK

"... at the tone, the time will be nine-twelve and twenty seconds, *kayn aynhoreh* ... at the tone, the time will be nine-twelve and thirty seconds, *kayn aynhoreh* ... at the tone, the time will be nine-twelve and forty seconds, *kayn aynhoreh* ..."

"Oh, she talks a lot . . . but only about her children."

"The Kitmans in 12-B. Tell them Elijah is here for the Seder."

"Well, they _are_, but now that you mention it, you know _you_ don't look Jewish _either_."

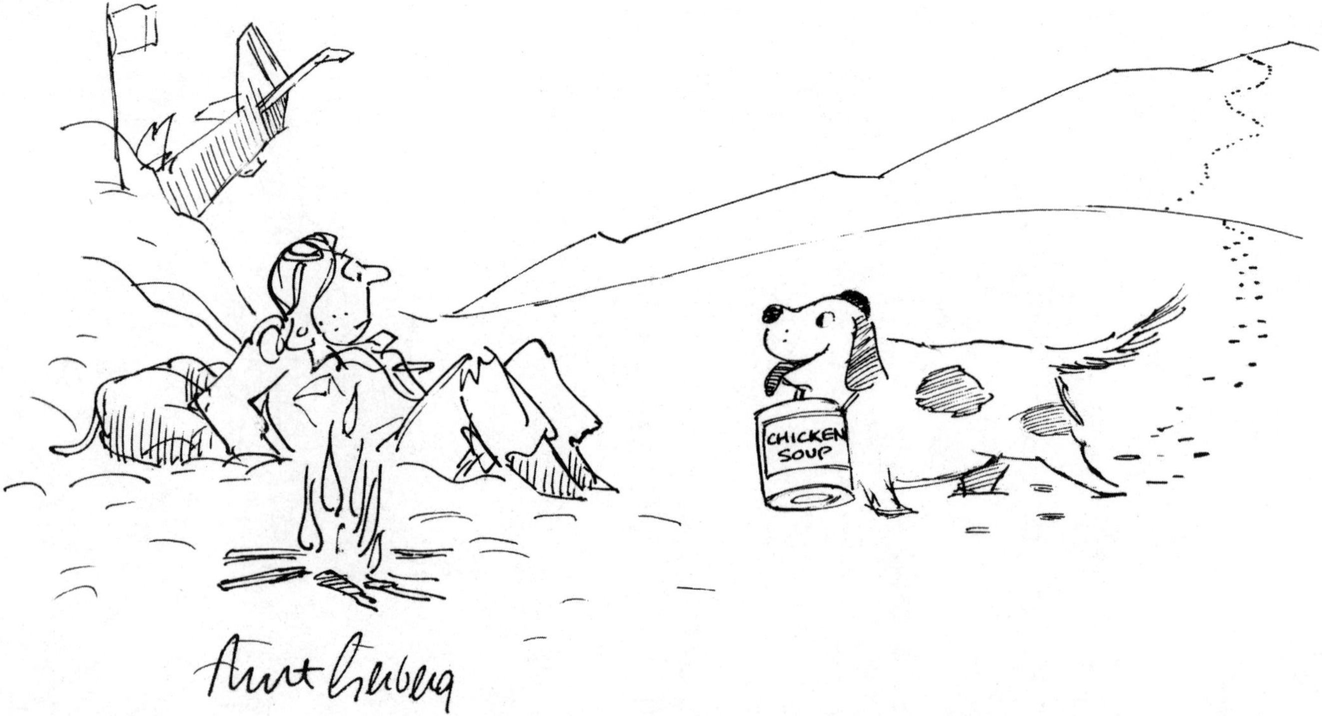
CHICKEN
SOUP

"So how about coming back to my place and I'll explain the Jewish dietary laws to you."

"Don't rush me! There's a very delicate line between good kitsch and junky *tchotchkes*."

"What? Me convert to Judaism? You crazy, man? I got enough tsoriss being a shvartzer!"

HIGH-TECH EVASION OF THE JEWISH MOTHER

"Sheldon is having a mid-life crisis. He can't decide whether to remain Reform, become Orthodox or return to Conservative."

"It's been over a year now—face facts—a prince, he's not."

"Listen, everybody: as a special treat, David will now read us several of his recent letters to The New York Times, chiding them for criticizing Israel."

"Don't knock Florida! Where else can a 73-year-old man get a 35-year mortgage?"

"And now, here's Dr. Frank Friedman to *kvetch* about the weather for you."

1.
WISHING WELL
2.
WISHING WELL
THANKS. I WISH YOU SHOULD ONLY LIVE AND BE WELL.

"Anyway, I bet there's a book in it."

"Let's make believe they have to get dressed to go out now because there's a big sale at Bloomingdale's."

". . . then there's the _cantor_ . . ."

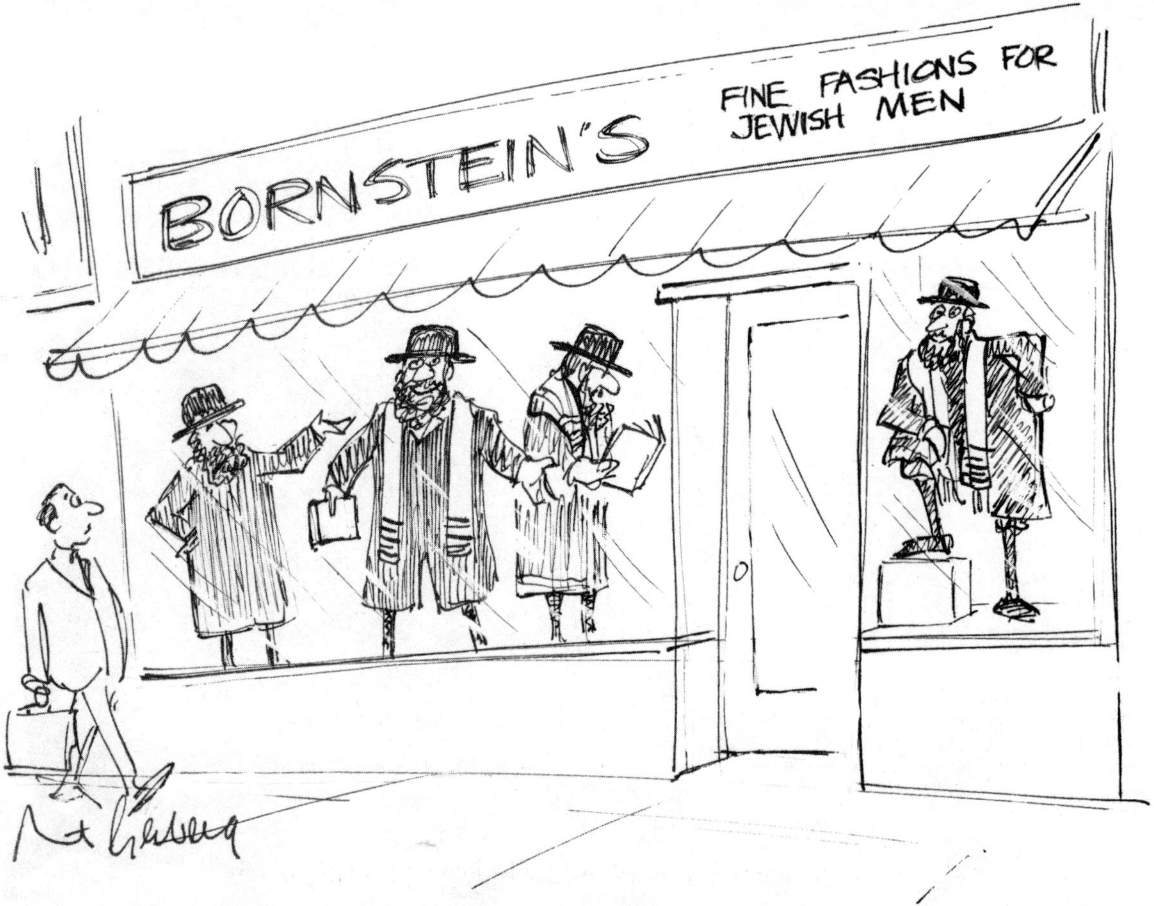
BORNSTEIN'S
FINE FASHIONS FOR
JEWISH MEN

"I appreciate your offer, but I was really hoping to marry a doctor."

"That by you is a _wish_? 'A toasted _bialy_ with _cream cheese_'?"

"Rachel! If you can't even stay focused on spreading peat moss, how do you expect to get into law school?"

"May I quote You?"

"Excuse me for sounding like a Jewish mother, but may I point out that your kid is getting wet."

THE FOLLOWING
RE-RUN
IS BROUGHT
TO YOU THROUGH
INCREDIBLE
CHUTZPA

"Actually, the neighborhood today is much less restricted than it used to be."

ORTHODOX CONGREGATION
TEMPLE SHARI OLOM
REFORM CONGREGATION

"No ham in this, I hope?"

"Oh, I'm so sorry! My mother always _said_ that skiing was not a thing for a _Jewish_ person."

WORST FEARS REALIZED: #18

"And the top story this Monday night is that Judy Solomon, of 693 East 78th Street, gained nine pounds over the weekend because she ate *trayf!*"

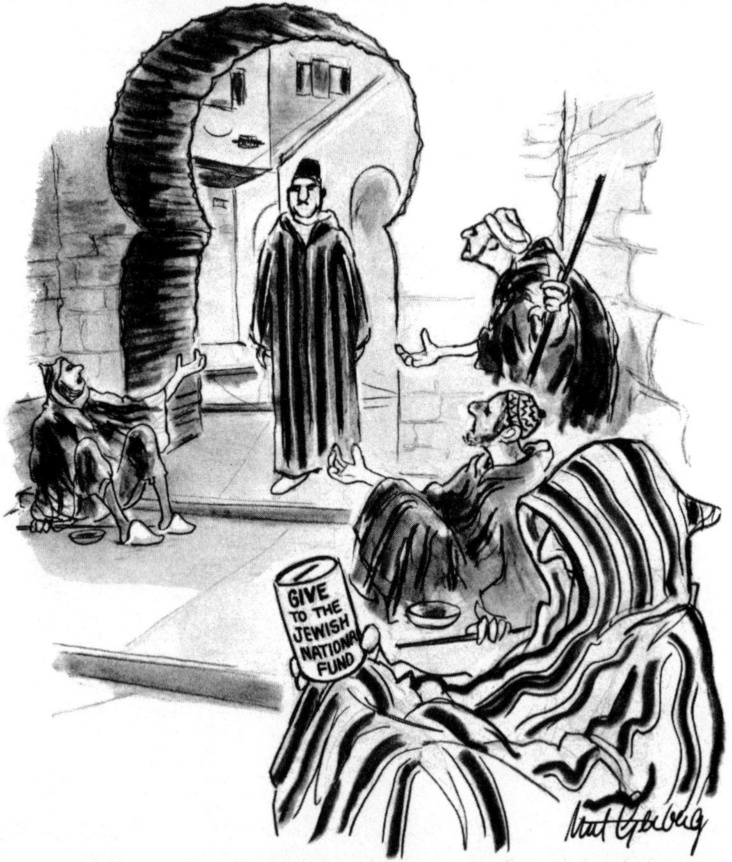
GIVE
TO THE
JEWISH
NATIONA
FUND

"I'd invite you back to the house for a glass of iced tea, but I'm afraid our kitchen isn't *kosher*."

THE SHNORRER'S SHNORRER

"The problem is that our ads have either been too Jewish or not Jewish enough."

"Are you *crazy*? A bacon and tomato *sandwich*? On *Yom Kippur*?"

"It's Barbra Streisand and I'm listening to her because she's Jewish so she puts me in the mood to practice my *Bat Mitzvah Haftorah*."

BUS
STOP
COOL
DISPOSITION
CHILLY
DEMEANOR
COLD
SHOULDER
FROZEN
STARE
AAAAH, SHE'S
PROBABLY NOT
EVEN JEWISH,
ANYWAY

"Meyerwitz, how long has it been since you've given me cause to shake your hand, pound you on the back and shout, 'Mazel Tov!'?"

"Well, there's still lots of water around, but alternate-side-of-the-street parking regulations have been suspended indefinitely."

"Some plastic surgeon did a marvelous job on your nose, Miss Levine. May I have the honor to do likewise for your gums?"

"'Happily ever after' you want? Then you keep the house kosher!"

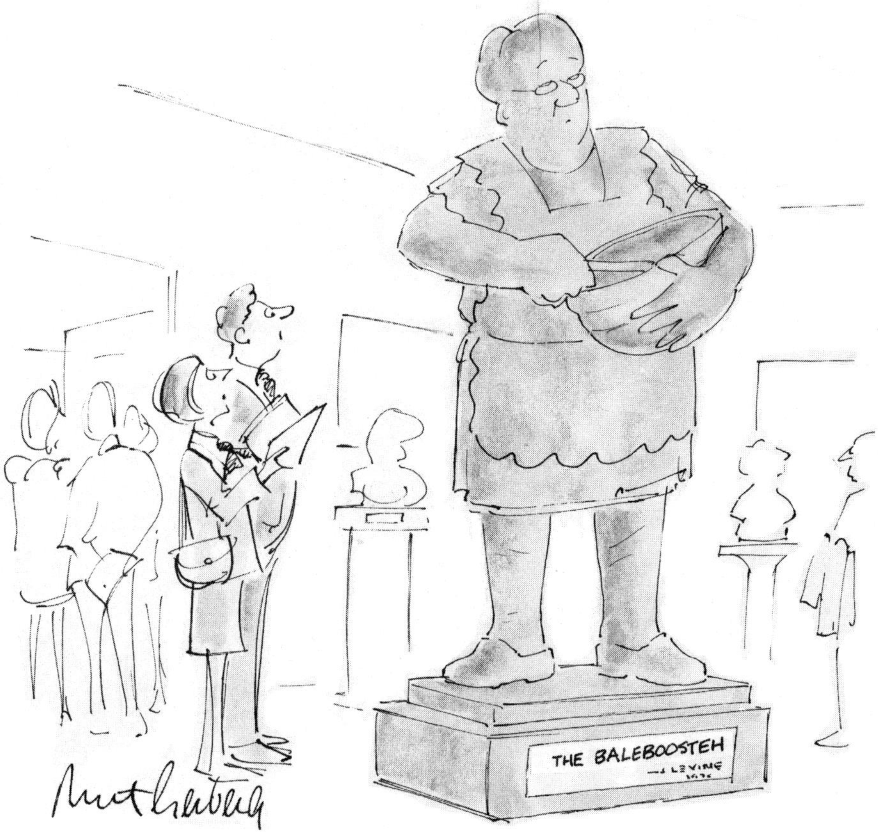
THE BALEBOOSTEH
J. LEVINE

"It is wonderful here. Except that I'm always in dread of gypsy moths and—since I'm not Jewish—frogs, vermin, flies, blood, pestilence, boils, hail, locusts, darkness and the slaying of my first born."

"So what do you think, Howie—will you still love me when I'm old and blonde?"

"And just why is this knight different from all other knights?"

baleboosteh *A most wonderfully accomplished all-round homemaker*
Bat Mitzvah *A religious ceremony marking a Jewish girl's attaining adulthood, at age 13*
bialy *A flat roll, usually made with onions*
broche *A blessing; a prayer of thanks and praise*
chutzpa *Total brazenness, insolence, audaciousness, arrogance*
gefilte fish *Traditional Jewish dish; a stuffed fish loaf*
goyim *People who are not Jewish*
goyish *Something that is not Jewish*
Haftorah *A chapter from the Prophets, read in the synagogue during the service*
kayn aynhoreh *Phrase used to protect against the evil eye: "You should live and be well, kayn aynhoreh (Thank God)."*
kosher *Permissible (to eat) according to Jewish dietary laws*
kvetch *To complain, fret, gripe*
matzos *Unleavened bread, eaten mainly during Passover*
mazel tov *"Good luck," but in common usage, "Congratulations"*
minyan *A quorum of ten male Jews needed to begin a prayer service*
mishegoss *Craziness, madness, insanity (primarily in a light vein)*
potchkeeing *Fussing, playing or messing around, unproductively*
Seder *Order of the service of the Passover dinner*

shaygetsers   *Men who are not Jewish*
shiksa   *A woman who is not Jewish, and especially young and attractive*
shnorrer   *A moocher, a brazen chiseler, a bum*
shul   *A house of prayer, a synagogue*
shvartzer   *A black man*
Talmud   *A collection of commentaries on the Bible*
tchotchke   *An object of small value, as a souvenir, toy or decoration*
trayf   *Food that is not kosher*
tsoriss   *Troubles, worries*
Yom Kippur   *Day of Atonement; the most holy day on the Jewish calendar*